Snuggle up in bed with these wonderful stories, and by the light of the full moon, find out about all the funny and fantastical, scary and strange things that happen at night. You won't want to go to sleep till you've read every story!

Every tale tucked up in this bed has been carefully chosen by children's book specialist Pat Thomson as ideal for five- to seven-year-olds. They are all by top favourite children's authors such as Dick King-Smith, James Reeves, Adèle Geras and Joan Aiken.

Pat Thomson is a well-known author and anthologist of children's stories. She also works with teachers as a lecturer and librarian. She is an Honorary Vice-President of the Federation of Children's Book Groups.

A Bed full of Night-time Stories

COLLECTED BY

Pat Thomson

CORGI BOOKS

A BED FULL OF NIGHT-TIME STORIES
A CORGI BOOK : 0 552 52961 3

PRINTING HISTORY
Corgi edition published 1998

Collection copyright © Pat Thomson, 1998
Illustrations copyright © Anthony Lewis, 1998

The right of Pat Thomson to be identified as the compiler of this work has
been asserted in accordance with the Copyright, Designs and Patents Act 1988

Set in 16/20pt Bembo Schoolbook by
Phoenix Typesetting, Ilkley, West Yorkshire

Corgi Books are published by Transworld Publishers Ltd,
61–63 Uxbridge Road, Ealing, London W5 5SA,
in Australia by Transworld Publishers (Australia) Pty. Ltd,
15–25 Helles Avenue, Moorebank, NSW 2170,
and in New Zealand by Transworld Publishers (NZ) Ltd,
3 William Pickering Drive, Albany, Auckland.

Printed and bound in Great Britain by
Cox & Wyman Ltd, Reading, Berkshire.

Acknowledgements

The editor and publisher are grateful for permission to include the following copyright stories:

Joan Aiken, 'The Patchwork Quilt' from *A Necklace of Raindrops* (Jonathan Cape, 1968), © Joan Aiken Enterprises Ltd.

Antonia Barber, 'The Shoes That Were Danced to Pieces' from *Tales from Grimm* (Frances Lincoln, 1992) by Antonia Barber, © 1992. Reproduced by permission of Frances Lincoln Ltd, 4 Torriano Mews, London NW5 2RZ.

Helen Cresswell, 'Lizzie Dripping by Moonlight' from *Silver Jackanory* (BBC Books, 1991), © Helen Creswell. Reprinted by permission of BBC Worldwide Limited.

Eleanor Farjeon, 'The Sea-Baby' from *The Old Nurse's Stocking Basket* (Oxford, 1931).

Adèle Geras, 'Singing Socks', © Adèle Geras 1998. Reproduced by permission of the Author.

Dick King-Smith, 'The Ghost at Codlin Castle' from *The Ghost at Codlin Castle and Other Stories*

(Viking, 1992) by Dick King-Smith. Reprinted by permission of A.P. Watt Ltd on behalf of Fox Busters Ltd.

Naomi Lewis, 'Vasilissa, Baba Yaga, and the Little Doll' from *The Silent Playmate* (Gollancz, 1979) by Naomi Lewis. Reprinted by permission of Naomi Lewis.

Philippa Pearce, 'In the Middle of the Night' from *What the Neighbours Did* (Kestrel Books, 1972) by Philippa Pearce, © Philippa Pearce, 1972. Reproduced by permission of Penguin Books Ltd.

James Reeves, 'How the Moon Began' (Abelard Schuman, 1971), © James Reeves. Reprinted by permission of the James Reeves Estate.

Jenny Wagner, 'The Werewolf Knight' from *Family Treasures and Other Bedtime Stories* first published as *The Macquarie Bedtime Story Book* by The Macquarie Library, Sydney, Australia. © Jenny Wagner, 1987

Contents

Contents

The Patchwork Quilt

Far in the north, where the snow falls
for three hundred days each year, and
all the trees are Christmas trees, there
was an old lady making patchwork.
Her name was Mrs Noot. She had
many, many little three-cornered
pieces of cloth – boxes full and baskets
full, bags full and bundles full, all the
colours of the rainbow. There were
red pieces and blue pieces, pink pieces
and golden pieces. Some had flowers
on, some were plain.

Mrs Noot sewed twelve pieces into a

star. Then she sewed the stars together to make bigger stars. And then she sewed *those* together. She sewed them with gold thread and silver thread and white thread and black thread.

What do you suppose she was making?

She was making a quilt for the bed of her little grandson Nils. She had nearly finished. When she had put in the last star, little Nils would have the biggest and brightest and warmest and most beautiful quilt in the whole of the north country – perhaps in the whole world.

While his granny sewed, little Nils sat beside her and watched the way her needle flashed in and out of the coloured pieces, making little tiny stitches.

Sometimes he said, 'Is it nearly done, Granny?'

He had asked her this question every day for a year. Each time he asked it, Mrs Noot would sing,

'Moon and candle
Give me your light,
Fire in the hearth
Burn clear, burn bright.

Needle fly swiftly,
Thread run fast,
Until the quilt
Is done at last.

The finest quilt
That ever was,
Made from more than
A thousand stars!'

This was a magic song, to help her sew quickly. While she sang it little Nils would sit silent on his stool, stroking the bright colours of the quilt. And the fire would stop crackling to listen, and the wind would hush its blowing.

Now the quilt was nearly done.

It would be ready in time for Nils's birthday.

Far, far to the south of Mrs Noot's cottage, in the hot, dry country where there is no grass and it rains only once every three years, a wizard lived in the desert. His name was Ali Beg.

Ali Beg was very lazy. All day he slept in the sun, lying on a magic carpet, while twelve camels stood round it, shading him. At night he went flying on his carpet. But even then the unhappy camels were not allowed to sit down. They had to stand in a square, each with a green lamp hanging on a chain round its neck, so that when Ali Beg came home he could see where to land in the dark.

The poor camels were tired out, and very hungry too, because they never had enough to eat.

As well as being unkind to his camels, Ali Beg was a thief. Everything he had was stolen – his clothes, his magic carpet, his camels, even the green lights on their necks. (They were really traffic lights; Ali Beg had stolen them from the city of Beirut one day as he flew over, so all the traffic had come to a stop.)

In a box Ali Beg kept a magic eye, which could see all the beautiful things everywhere in the world. Every night he looked into the eye and chose something new to steal.

One day when Ali Beg was lying fast asleep, the eldest of the camels said, 'Friends, I am faint with hunger.

I must have something to eat.'

The youngest camel said, 'As there is no grass, let us eat the carpet.'

So they began to nibble the edge of the carpet. It was thick and soft and silky. They nibbled and nibbled, they munched and munched, until there was nothing left but the bit under Ali Beg.

When he woke up he was very angry.

'Wicked camels! You have ruined my carpet! I am going to beat you with my umbrella and you shall have no food for a year. Now I have all the trouble of finding another carpet.'

When he had beaten the camels, Ali Beg took his magic eye out of its box.

He said to it:

'Find me a carpet
Magic Eye,
To carry me far
And carry me high.'

Then he looked into the magic
eye to see what he could see. The
eye went dark, and then it went
bright.

What Ali Beg could see then was
the kitchen of Mrs Noot's cottage.
There she sat, by her big fireplace,
sewing away at the wonderful
patchwork quilt.

'Aha!' said Ali Beg. 'I can see that
is a magic quilt – just the thing for
me.'

He jumped on what was left of the
magic carpet. He had to sit astride,
the way you do on a horse, because
there was so little left.

'Carry me, carpet,
Carry me fast,
Through burning sun,
Through wintry blast.

With never a slip
And never a tilt,
Carry me straight
To the magic quilt.'

The piece of carpet carried him up
into the air. But it was so small that it
could not go very fast. In fact it went
so slowly that as it crept along, Ali
Beg was burned black by the hot sun.
Then, when he came to the cold
north country where Mrs Noot lived,
he was frozen by the cold.

By now night had fallen. The
carpet was going slower and slower
and slower – lower and lower and
lower. At last it sank down on a

mountain top. It was quite worn out. Ali Beg angrily stepped off and walked down the mountain to Mrs Noot's house.

He looked through the window.

Little Nils was in bed fast asleep. Tomorrow would be his birthday.

Mrs Noot had sat up late to finish the quilt. There was only one star left to put in. But she had fallen asleep in her chair, with the needle halfway through a patch.

Ali Beg softly lifted the latch.

He tiptoed in.

Very, very gently, so as not to wake Mrs Noot, he pulled the beautiful red and blue and green and crimson and pink and gold quilt from under her hands. He never noticed the needle. Mrs Noot never woke up.

Ali Beg stole out of the door, carrying the quilt.

He spread it out on the snow. Even in the moonlight, its colours showed bright.

Ali Beg sat down on it. He said,

'By hill and dale,
Over forest and foam
Carry me safely,
Carry me home!'

Old Mrs Noot had stitched a lot of magic into the quilt as she sewed and sang. It was even better than the carpet. It rose up into the air and carried Ali Beg south, towards the hot country.

When Mrs Noot woke and found her beautiful quilt gone, she and little Nils hunted for it everywhere, but it was not in the kitchen – nor in the woodshed – nor in the forest – nowhere.

Although it was his birthday, little Nils cried all day.

Back in the desert, Ali Beg lay down on the quilt and went to sleep. The camels stood round, shading him.

Then the youngest camel said, 'Friends, I have been thinking. Why should we keep the sun off this wicked man while he sleeps on a soft quilt? Let us roll him onto the sand and sit on the quilt ourselves. Then we can make it take us away and leave him behind.'

Three camels took hold of Ali Beg's clothes with their teeth and pulled him off the quilt. Then they all sat on it in a ring, round the star-shaped hole in the middle. (Luckily it was a *very* big quilt.)

The eldest camel said,

'Beautiful quilt,
So fine and grand,
Carry us home
To your native land.'

At once the quilt rose up in the air,
with all the camels sitting on it.

At that moment, Ali Beg woke. He
saw them up above him. With a shout
of rage, he jumped up and made a
grab for the quilt. His fingers just
caught in the star-shaped hole.

The quilt sailed along with Ali Beg
hanging underneath.

The youngest camel said, 'Friends,
let us get rid of Ali Beg. He is too
heavy for this quilt.'

So all the camels humped and
bumped and thumped, they knocked
and rocked, they slipped and tipped,

they wriggled and jiggled, until the needle which Mrs Noot had left sticking through a patch ran into Ali Beg's finger. He gave a yell and let go. He fell down and down, down and down and down, until he hit the sea with a great SPLASH.

And that was the end of Ali Beg.

But the quilt sailed on, with the camels. As they flew over Beirut, they threw down the twelve green traffic lights.

When at last they landed outside Mrs Noot's house, Nils came running out.

'Oh, Granny!' he cried. 'Come and see! The quilt has come back! And it has brought me twelve camels for a birthday present.'

'Dear me,' said Mrs Noot, 'I shall have to make them jackets, or they will find it too cold in these parts.'

So she made them beautiful patchwork jackets and gave them plenty of hot porridge to eat. The camels were very happy to have found such a kind home.

Mrs Noot sewed the last star into the patchwork and spread the quilt on Nils's bed.

'There,' she said. 'Now it's bedtime!'

Nils jumped into bed and lay proudly under his beautiful quilt. He went straight to sleep. And what wonderful dreams he had that night, and every night after, while his granny sat in front of the big fire, with six camels on either side of her.

This story is by Joan Aiken.

Singing Socks

Cath woke up suddenly in the night.

'Ronnie? Nibbles? Are you awake?
I've remembered Three Horrible
Things.'

Ronnie was a hand-made panda.
Her stuffing had thinned out over the
years, and now she was flabby and
floppy and rested against the
headboard. Nibbles was a brown-
and-white furry dog with one missing
ear, who kept Ronnie company on
Cath's bed. They spoke to her at
night, or whenever she was sad, and
Cath had kept this secret all to herself.

24

Not even Clare, her big sister, knew about Ronnie and Nibbles.

'She probably thinks,' Cath told them, 'that it's just me, talking to myself.'

'What are the Three Horrible Things you've remembered?' Ronnie asked now.

'Number One: Clare has gone to stay at Shahnaz's house, and that means the top bunk is empty. Number Two: Mum and Dad have gone out till late in the night, and Number Three is the worst of the lot: Mrs Batsford is baby-sitting. She must be down there this very minute.'

'You knew those Horrible Things before you went to sleep,' said Nibbles, who was a dog filled with common sense, even though one of his ears had fallen off in the washing-machine.

'They weren't horrible then,' said Cath, 'because it was still light. Lots of things only get horrible in the dark.'

'I like the dark,' said Ronnie. 'I like to see the Moonclock all lit up.'

'Yes,' said Cath, looking at the nightlight on her bedside table, which had a Man-in-the-Moon face and glowed pale green in the darkness. 'I like the Moonclock too, but there might be Something up there in Clare's bunk.'

'What, for instance?' asked Ronnie.

'A Dinosaur?' Cath suggested. 'Or a Giant Monster?'

'Go and have a look,' said Nibbles. 'That's the best way to deal with Horrible Things. Go and look at 'em, I always say. I'll come up with you and keep you company.'

'I'm scared,' said Cath. 'What if we find Something?'

'We'll scream,' said Nibbles. 'Very loudly indeed. Mrs Batsford will come. We'll scream so loudly that all the neighbours will hear.'

So Cath took Nibbles under one arm and climbed up the ladder to Clare's bunk. Clare's dolls sat in a row leaning against the wall, staring at Cath out of glass eyes, but she was used to that. There were no Dinosaurs or Giant Monsters on the bed, but there was a Sinister Lump under the quilt, just by the pillow.

'What's that?' Cath whispered.

'Pull the quilt back and have a look,' said Nibbles 'and I'll get ready to scream.'

Cath closed her eyes tight and pulled the quilt back. When she opened them, all she found was Clare's My Little Pony, wrapped in a mauve silk scarf.

'It's only Dorabella,' said Cath to Nibbles. 'Let's climb down again.'

'There,' said Ronnie, when Cath was safely back in her own bed. 'A lot of fuss about nothing.'

'That still leaves,' said Cath, 'two Horrible Things.'

'Your mum and dad being out is not a Horrible Thing,' said Nibbles. 'It's a Very Nice Thing. It's probably a Treat.'

'Only for them,' said Cath. 'It's not a treat for me. Everyone else is having a treat tonight except me. It's not fair.'

'You went to stay the night with your friend Heather,' said Ronnie, 'just the other day. You hated it.'

'The food was funny,' said Cath. 'Full of bits and shreds. You couldn't see what anything really was. And I didn't have anyone to chat to at night.'

'You should have taken us,' said Nibbles. 'Me and Ronnie.'

'I know,' said Cath. 'I forgot to put you in my bag. I'm sorry.' This wasn't quite true. Cath hadn't packed her cuddly toys because she wanted to appear grown-up, but she wasn't going to tell Ronnie and Nibbles that. Their feelings might be hurt. She said, 'Mum and Dad could have taken me with them to the Crowthers' house. I could have slept on a bed upstairs till it was time to come home.'

'They did that once, remember?' said Ronnie. Cath *did* remember. Mum and Dad had been cross. They said she'd wrecked the whole party. Cath thought that was a cruel thing to say. It wasn't *her* fault that she couldn't get to sleep, and kept coming downstairs and eating bits from

Mum's plate, and most of the after-dinner peppermint creams. The grown-ups had been making too much noise. When she had told Mum this, the only reply had been, 'I'm getting a baby-sitter from now on and that's that.'

'Well,' said Ronnie soothingly, 'if anything really dreadful happens, Mrs Batsford will phone your parents and they'll come back.'

'Could I call them back if I'm scared?'

'What are you scared of?' asked Nibbles.

'Stuff,' said Cath. 'All sorts of stuff. I don't like those Shapes on the chest of drawers.'

'Those are your ornaments,' said Ronnie.

'In the daytime,' said Cath. 'At night, they're Shapes. They're dark and spooky. I also don't like the Creature on the Hook. There, behind the door.'

'That's your dressing-gown,' said Nibbles.

'There might be a Creature *in* the dressing-gown,' said Cath. 'Wrapped up in it.'

'Let's go and see,' said Ronnie. So Cath tucked Ronnie under her arm and tiptoed over to the door.

'I'll get ready to scream,' said Ronnie.

Cath patted the dressing-gown all over and felt nothing but cloth under her hands. If there *was* a Creature in her dressing-gown, it was the very flat, wispy kind and they didn't count. Cath went back to bed.

'The Third Horrible Thing,' she said, 'is worst of all. Mrs Batsford is downstairs.'

'What's wrong with that?' asked Nibbles.

'Everyone thinks she's a nice old lady,' said Cath 'but Clare and Shahnaz told me something awful about her. At night, she turns into a bat and flits about.' Cath considered this. She imagined Mrs Batsford sitting downstairs on the sofa with her velvety black wings carefully folded behind her, ready to fly up the stairs to this very bedroom if Cath made any noise at all. But what if she needed something? What if a terrible stomach-ache arrived? What if she desperately wanted a glass of water? As Cath thought about it more and more, her stomach *did* begin to feel a little uncomfortable, and suddenly a drink of cold water was what she felt like more than anything.

'And I can't have one!' she howled.

'I can never have a glass of water. If I call Mrs Batsford, she'll come up here and be a bat and flit about.' Tears ran down Cath's cheeks, and collected in small puddles round her neck and behind her ears.

'Is anything the matter, dear?' Cath recognized Mrs Batsford's voice and looked over to the door. There, outlined against the light coming from the landing stood an unmistakeable BAT! Cath could see huge, dark wings . . . she screamed and turned to bury her face in the pillow.

Mrs Batsford turned the light on and walked over to the bed.

'Cathleen, darling, whatever's the matter? Are you having a nightmare?'

Cath opened her eyes. It was safe to do this now that the light was on. Mrs Batsford's wings turned out to be a tartan shawl, and the old lady was

smiling so kindly at her that Cath instantly felt ashamed of all the Bat-thoughts she'd been having.

'I was scared,' said Cath. 'That's all.'

'Goodness,' said Mrs Batsford. 'Whatever could have frightened you in your very own bedroom?'

Out of the corner of her eye, Cath could see her socks dangling over the back of the chair. They looked a little like snakes. She said, 'It was my socks. I thought they were snakes. They looked quite wriggly in the dark.'

'Oh, they can,' Mrs Batsford agreed. 'My long stockings are even worse. I often roll mine up at night. That keeps them in their place. But your socks are the very best possible kind you could have. They're Singing Socks.'

'I've never heard,' said Cath, 'of Singing Socks.'

'They *are* rare,' said Mrs Batsford. 'I grant you that. I haven't seen a pair for a good many years, but once you learn how to spot them, they're easy to recognize. It's the bows, you see. A sock with a bow on it will probably turn out to be a reasonably good singer. Let's see what we can get out of this pair.'

'May I have a drink of water before we begin?' Cath asked.

'Certainly, dear,' said Mrs Batsford.

After she had taken the glass back to the bathroom, Mrs Batsford came back to Cath's bedroom and turned out the light. Her shawl flapped rather alarmingly as she made her way back to the bed, but Cath forced herself to remember it was only fluffy squares of red, yellow and black.

'Do we have to have the light off?' she asked. 'I don't care, really, but Ronnie and Nibbles are a little frightened of the dark.'

'Please explain to Ronnie and Nibbles that Singing Socks are extremely shy. Usually, they will only sing in complete darkness, but tonight, as a special favour to Ronnie and Nibbles, they will do their best to perform in the light of your splendid Moonclock.'

'There you are,' said Cath to Ronnie and Nibbles. 'It'll be OK. Just sit back and enjoy the song.' Ronnie flopped over and laid her head next to Cath's head on the pillow. Nibbles pricked his remaining ear and sat up very straight against the headboard. Mrs Batsford had taken Cath's socks from the chair and laid them over her lap.

'It's hard to sit on a bottom bunk,' she said 'so I shall perch over here.' She settled herself on the toy chest, which was a tin trunk covered by an old tablecloth.

Cath closed her eyes, just for a moment, and when she opened them again, the Socks had come to life. They seemed to be peeping out of Mrs Batsford's shawl, in the place where her hands should have been.

'You've put your hands into them,' Cath murmured, and Mrs Batsford said:

'Sssh! They're ready to sing. Close your eyes and listen for the magic, calming, Sock voices singing Ancient Songs from the Land of Socks.'

Cath closed her eyes and listened to the song:

> *'Socks who can sing are a great surprise.*

We are the Closers of everyone's eyes.
We are the Soothers of sorrowful cries.
Socks are the Singers of Lullabies.

We sing the song of the Serpent Socks,
who wriggle and bask on the turquoise
    rocks,
who turn their keys in the Golden
    Locks
and tell the time on their Sugar
    Clocks.'

If there was another verse, Cath
and Ronnie and Nibbles didn't hear it,
because they were fast asleep.

The next day, as she dressed, Cath
looked closely at her socks. She held
them up to her ears, but heard
nothing at all.

At breakfast, Mum said: 'Hello,
Cath. Mrs Batsford told me you were

as good as gold last night. No trouble at all.'

'I like Mrs Batsford,' said Cath. 'Will you go out again tonight?'

'Not tonight,' said Mum 'but soon. Should I ask Mrs Batsford to baby-sit again?'

'Yes, please,' said Cath. 'She . . .'

'She what?' asked Mum.

'Nothing. It doesn't matter.' Cath decided to keep the Singing Socks a secret. She would have to tell Clare because she would probably be in the top bunk next time Mrs Batsford came. Ronnie and Nibbles knew of course, but apart from them, Cath wasn't going to tell anyone else. The Singing Socks were shy. Mrs Batsford had said so.

This story is by Adèle Geras.

40

Vasilissa, Baba Yaga, and the Little Doll

In a far-off land in a far-off time, on the edge of a great forest, lived a girl named Vasilissa. Ah, poor Vasilissa! She was no more than eight years old when her mother died. But she had a friend, and that one was better than most. Who was this friend? A doll. As the mother lay ill she had called the child to her bedside. 'Vasilissa,' she said, 'here is a little doll. Take good care of her, and whenever you are in great need, give her some food and ask for her help; she will tell you what to do. Take her, with my blessing; but remember, she is your secret; no-one else must know of her at all. Now I can die content.'

The father of Vasilissa grieved for a time, then married a new wife, thinking that she would care for the little girl. But did she indeed! She had two daughters of her own, and not one of the three had a grain of love for Vasilissa. From early dawn to the last light of day, in the hot sun or the icy wind, they kept her toiling at all the hardest tasks, in or out of the house; never did she have a word of thanks. Yet whatever they set her to do was done, and done in time. For when she truly needed help she would set her doll on a ledge or table, give her a little food and drink, and tell the doll her troubles. With her help all was done.

One day in the late autumn the father had to leave for the town, a journey of many days. He set off at earliest dawn.

Darkness fell early. Rain beat on the cottage windows; the wind howled down the chimney – just the time for the wife to work a plan she had in mind. To each of the girls she gave a task: the first was set to making lace, the second to knitting stockings, Vasilissa to spinning.

'No stirring from your place, my girls, before you have done,' said the woman. Then, leaving them a single candle, she went to bed.

The three worked on for a while, but the light was small, and flickered. One sister pretended to trim the wick and it went out altogether – just as the mother had planned.

'Now we're in trouble,' said the

girl. 'For where's the new light to come from?'

'There's only one place,' said her sister, 'and that's from Baba Yaga.'

'That's right,' said the other. 'But who's to go?

> 'My needles shine;
> the job's not mine.'

'I can manage too,' said the other.

> 'My lace-pins shine;
> the job's not mine.

Vasilissa must go.'

'Yes, Vasilissa must go!' they cried together. And they pushed her out of the door.

Now who was Baba Yaga? She was a mighty witch; her hut was set on claws, like the legs of giant hens.

She rode in a mortar over the highest mountains, speeding it on with the pestle, sweeping away her traces with a broom. And she would crunch up in a trice any human who crossed her path.

But Vasilissa had a friend, and that one better than most. She took the doll from her pocket, and set some bread before her. 'Little doll,' she said, 'they are sending me into the forest to fetch a light from Baba Yaga's hut – and who has ever returned from there? Help me, little doll.'

The doll ate, and her eyes grew bright as stars. 'Have no fear,' said she. 'While I am with you nothing can do you harm. But remember – no-one else must know of your secret. Now let us start.'

How dark it was in the forest of towering trees! How the leaves hissed, how the branches creaked and moaned in the wind! But Vasilissa walked resolutely on, hour after hour. Suddenly, the earth began to tremble and a horseman thundered by. Both horse and rider were glittering white, hair and mane, swirling cloak and bridle too; and as they passed, the sky showed the first white light of dawn.

Vasilissa journeyed on, then again she heard a thundering noise, and a second horse and rider flashed into sight. Both shone red as scarlet, red as flame, swirling cloak and bridle too; as they rode beyond her view, the sun rose high. It was day.

On she walked, on and on, until she reached a clearing in the woods. In the centre was a hut – but the hut had feet; and they were the claws of hens. It was Baba Yaga's home, no doubt about that. All around was a fence of bones, and the posts were topped with skulls: a fearful sight in the fading light! And as she gazed, a third horseman thundered past; but this time horse and rider were black and black, swirling cloak and bridle too. They vanished into the gloom, and it was night. But, as darkness fell, the eyes of the skulls lit up like lamps and everything in the glade could be seen as sharp as day.

Swish! Swoosh! Varoom! Varoom! As Vasilissa stood there, frozen stiff with fear, a terrible noise came from over the forest. The wind screeched, the leaves hissed – Baba Yaga was riding home in her huge mortar, using her pestle as an oar, sweeping away the traces with her broom. At the gate of the hut she stopped and sniffed the air with her long nose.

'Phoo! Phoo! I smell Russian flesh!'

she croaked. 'Who's there? Out you come!'

Vasilissa took courage, stepped forward and made a low curtsey.

'It is I, Vasilissa. My sisters sent me for a light, since ours went out.'

'Oh, so that's it!' said the witch. 'I know those girls, and their mother too. Well, nothing's for nothing, as they say; you must work for me for a while, then we'll see about the light.' She turned to the hut and sang in a high shrill screech:

> 'Open gates! Open gates!
> Baba Yaga waits.'

The weird fence opened; the witch seized the girl's arm in her bony fingers and pushed her into the hut. 'Now,' said she, 'get a light from the lamps outside,' – she meant the skulls

– 'and serve my supper. It's in the oven, and the soup's in the cauldron there.' She lay down on a bench while Vasilissa carried the food to the table until she was quite worn out, but she dared not stop. And the witch devoured more than ten strong men could have eaten – whole geese and hens and roasted pigs; loaf after loaf; huge buckets of beer and wine, cider and Russian kvass. At last, all that remained was a crust of bread.

'There's your supper, girl,' said the witch. 'But you must earn it, mind; I don't like greed. While I'm off tomorrow you must clear out the yard; it hasn't been touched for years, and it quite blocks out the view. Then you must sweep the hut, wash the linen, cook the dinner – and mind you cook enough; I was half-starved tonight. Then – for I'll have no lazybones around – there's another little job. You see that sack? It's full of black beans, wheat and poppy seed, some other things too, I dare say. Sort them out into their separate lots, and if a single one is out of place, woe betide! Into the cauldron you shall go, and I'll crunch you up for breakfast in a trice.'

So saying, she lay down by the stove and was instantly fast asleep. Snorrre . . . Snorrre . . . It was a horrible sound.

Vasilissa took the doll from her pocket and gave her the piece of bread. 'Little doll,' said she. 'How am I to do all these tasks? Or even one of them? How can a little doll like you help now? We are lost indeed.'

'Vasilissa,' said the doll. 'Again I tell you, have no fear. Say your prayers and go to sleep. Tomorrow knows what is hidden from yesterday.'

She slept – but she woke early, before the first glimmer of day. Where should she start on the mountain of work? Then she heard a thundering of hoofs; white horse and white rider flashed past the window – suddenly it was dawn. The light in the skulls' eyes dwindled and went out. Then the poor girl hid in the shadows, for she saw Baba Yaga get to her feet – Creak! Creak! – and shuffle to the door. There, the witch gave a piercing whistle, and mortar, pestle and broom came hurtling towards her, stopping where she stood. In she stepped, off she rode, over tree-tops, through the clouds, using the pestle like an oar, sweeping away her traces with the broom. Just as she soared away, the red horse and red rider thundered past: suddenly it was

day, and the sun shone down.

Vasilissa turned away from the window, but what was this? She could not believe her eyes.

Every task was done. The yard was cleared, the linen washed, the grains and the seeds were all in separate bins, the dinner was set to cook. And there was the little doll, waiting to get back in her pocket. 'All you need to do,' said the doll, 'is to set the table and serve it all, hot and hot, when she returns. But keep your wits about you all the same, for she's a sly one.'

The winter daylight faded fast; again there was a thundering of hoofs; black horse, black rider sped through the glade and were gone. Darkness fell, and the eyes of the skulls once more began to glow. And then, with a swish and a roar, down swept the mortar, out stepped Baba Yaga.

'Well, girl, why are you standing idle? You know what I told you.'

'The work is all done, Granny.'

Baba Yaga looked and looked but done it all was. So she sat down, grumbling and mumbling, to eat her supper. It was good, very good: it put her in a pleasant humour, for a witch.

'Tell me, girl, why do you sit there as if you were dumb?'

'Granny, I did not dare to speak – but, now, if you permit it, may I ask a question?'

'Ask if you will, but remember that not every question leads to good. The more you know, the older you grow.'

'Well, Granny, can you tell me, who is the white rider on the white horse, the one who passed at dawn?'

'He is my Bright Morning, and

he brings the earliest light.'

'Then who is the rider all in red on the flame-red horse?'

'Ah, he is my Fiery Sun and brings the day.'

'And who is the horseman all in black on the coal-black horse?'

'He is my Dark Night. All are my faithful servants. Now I shall ask *you* a question; mind you answer me properly. How did you do all those tasks I set you?'

Vasilissa recalled her mother's words, never to tell the secret of the doll.

'My mother gave me a blessing before she died, and that helps me when in need.'

'A blessing! I want no blessed children here! Out you get! Away! Away!' And she pushed her through the door. 'You've earned your pay –

now take it.' She took down one of the gatepost skulls, fixed it on a stick, and thrust it into Vasilissa's hand. 'Now – off!'

Vasilissa needed no second bidding. She hastened on, her path now lit by the eyes of the fearful lamp. And so, at last, she was home.

'Why have you taken so long?' screamed the mother and the sisters. They had been in darkness ever since she left. They had gone in every direction to borrow a light, but once it was inside in the house, every flame went out. So they seized the skull with joy.

But the glaring eyes stared back; wherever they turned they could not escape the scorching rays. Soon, all that remained of the three was a little ash. Then the light of the skull went out for ever; its task was done.

Vasilissa buried it in the garden, and a bush of red roses sprang up on the spot. She did not fear to be alone, for the little doll kept her company. And when her father returned, rejoicing to see her, this tale she told him, just as it has been told to you.

This story is a Russian folk tale, re-told by Naomi Lewis.

The Ghost at Codlin Castle

'Gran,' said Peter as his grandmother was tucking him up in bed, 'd'you believe in ghosts?'

'Oh yes,' said his grandmother.

'So d'you know a good ghost story to tell me?'

'Now?'

'Yes.'

'All right.'

Like a great many ghosts (said Gran), Sir Anthony Appleby was wary of people. It wasn't that they could do him any harm. That had been done

58

ages ago. It was the fuss they made when they came upon him, in the winding corridors and steep stone stairways of Codlin Castle.

Some screamed and ran, some stood rooted to the spot, trembling and ashen-faced, some fainted. But no-one ever said a kind word to him. In fact, no-one had spoken a word of any kind to him since his death in 1588. In time past, things had not been so bad, for then the only inhabitants of Codlin Castle had been the Appleby family and their servants; all were quite used to the ghost of Sir Anthony, and though they may not have spoken to him, at least they were no trouble to him.

Nowadays things were different, for the Appleby fortunes had dwindled over the centuries, until finally one of Sir Anthony's descendants had been forced to sell the family seat.

Now it was known as the Codlin Castle Hotel, where well-to-do folk came to stay, to sleep in canopied four-posters and to eat rich meals in the medieval Banqueting Hall. Sir Anthony kept bumping into them in the corridors and stairways, and all of them, it seemed, were frightened of ghosts.

'A fellow can't get any peace these days,' said Sir Anthony grumpily (like all ghosts, he talked to himself a great deal). 'One look at me and they lose their heads,' and then he allowed himself a smile, for though dressed in the costume of his age − doublet and hose, flowing cloak, high ruffed collar, sword by his side − he was, as always, carrying his head underneath one arm.

For three hundred and forty-two

years he had carried it thus, ever since that fateful day when, as one of her courtiers, he had accompanied Queen Elizabeth on a visit to her fleet at Tilbury.

On the dockside there was a large puddle, and the Queen stopped before it.

'Your cloak, Sir Anthony,' she said.

Sir Anthony hesitated.

'Majesty?' he said.

'I may have the heart and stomach of a king,' said Queen Elizabeth, 'but I have the feet of a weak and feeble woman and I don't want to get them wet. Cast your cloak upon yonder puddle.'

'But Your Majesty,' said Sir Anthony Appleby, 'it is a brand-new cloak and it will get all muddy,' at which the Queen ordered that he be taken straight away to the Tower of

London and there beheaded, while Sir Walter Raleigh hastily threw down his own cloak.

The years and indeed the centuries slipped by. One sultry summer's night in 1930, the stable clock was striking twelve as the ghost made his way along a stone-flagged passageway in the West Wing, his head tucked underneath his left arm. This was how he usually carried it, to leave his sword arm free, though sometimes he changed sides for the head was quite heavy. Once, a couple of hundred years ago, he had tried balancing it on top of his neck, just for fun, but this had not been a success. A serving wench had come upon him suddenly in the castle kitchens, making him jump so that the head fell off and rolled along the floor, at which the wretched girl, a newcomer, had died of fright.

Remembering this incident as the twelfth stroke sounded, Sir Anthony stopped opposite a tall cheval-glass standing in the passage, and taking up his head with both hands, set it carefully above the great ruffed collar.

'A fine figure of a man,' he remarked to his reflection, 'though I say it myself,' and, pressing his palms against his ears to keep the head steady, he turned this way and that, the better to admire himself. He could not therefore hear the approach of soft footsteps, but suddenly saw, beside his own reflection, that of a small girl in pink pyjamas.

'Hello,' she said. 'Who are you?'

So startled was Sir Anthony that he almost dropped his head.

'My . . . my name is . . . is Sir Anthony Appleby,' he stammered, turning to face the child. 'And who, pray, are you, young miss?'

'I'm Biffy,' said the small girl. 'It's short for Elizabeth.'

That name again, thought Sir Anthony, but at least someone's spoken to me at last.

'Why aren't you in bed?' he said.

'Too hot,' said Biffy. 'I couldn't sleep. Why aren't you?'

'Oh, I never sleep,' said Sir Anthony. 'I'm a ghost, you see.'

'What fun,' said Biffy. 'How long have you been dead?'

'Three hundred and forty-two years.'

'Oh. So that's why you're wearing those funny clothes.'

'Yes.'

'Why have you got your hands pressed to your ears? Have you the earache?'

'No, no,' said Sir Anthony. 'Ghosts can't feel pain. It's about the only advantage of being one.'

'Then why are you holding your head?' said Biffy.

Oh dear, thought the ghost. If I take off my head, the child will scream or faint or even die of fright. And I do so want her to say a kind word to me. One kind word and I'm sure I could rest in peace at long last, instead of having to trudge round these winding corridors and steep stone stairways for the rest of my death.

'Look,' he said. 'If I tell you a secret, will you promise faithfully not to scream or faint or die of fright?'

'I promise.'

'Well, you see, when I died, it was in a rather unusual way. I mean, it was common enough then, but they

65

don't do it nowadays.'

'What did they do to you?'

'They executed me. They cut off my head. That's why I'm holding it like this now. I'm just balancing it, you see. It's not attached.'

'What fun,' said Biffy. 'Take it off.'

The ghost's face wore a very worried expression.

'You promised not to scream or faint or die of fright, remember?' he said.

'Yes,' said Biffy. 'Don't worry.'

So Sir Anthony Appleby removed his head, holding it carefully by its long hair, and tucked it under his arm.

The small girl in the pink pyjamas clapped her hands in delight.

'That's wonderful!' she said, and at these words a broad grin of pleasure spread over the bearded features.

'Oh, Sir Anthony Appleby,' said Biffy. 'You really are the nicest ghost in the whole wide world!' and because she was just the right height, she gave him a kiss on the top of his head.

Immediately the ghost of Codlin Castle vanished.

Biffy looked all around, but there was no sign of him.

She looked in the cheval-glass, but saw only her own reflection, standing there in her pink pyjamas.

So she went back to bed.

'Is that the end of the story?' said Peter.

'Yes, I suppose it is,' said his grandmother. 'Except that from then onward, nobody at the Codlin Castle Hotel ever saw the ghost of Sir Anthony Appleby again.'

'Because he was at peace at last, you mean?'

'Yes.'

'Because the girl said a kind word to him?'

'Yes.'

'Gran,' said Peter. 'Your name's Elizabeth, isn't it?'

'Yes. But when I was little, I was always called Biffy.'

This story is by Dick King-Smith.

The Shoes That Were Danced to Pieces

Long ago, in a far land, lived a king with twelve beautiful daughters. Each night they slept in twelve silken beds, all in the same great bedroom and once they were all in bed, the king closed the great doors and bolted them. Yet every morning, when the doors were opened, he found his daughters tired and yawning and their dainty shoes quite worn out as if they had been dancing all night.

Try as he might, the king could not

discover how this came about. At last, he proclaimed that any man who could solve the mystery might choose whichever princess he wished to be his wife, and that he should be the next king in that land. But to discourage every Tom, Dick and Harry from trying his luck, and wasting the king's time, he added that anyone who tried and could not give an answer after three nights, should find his life forfeit.

In spite of this, many men came seeking the prize: kings' sons, brave warriors, and men famed for their wisdom; but none could find the answer and all met with the same sorry fate. As time passed, fewer and fewer came, for it began to be whispered that the princesses were skilled in magic and that no man could find out their secret.

It happened at last that a poor

soldier came into that land. He had
been wounded in battle and could no
longer serve, but limped along the
highroad towards the city, where the
king and the twelve princesses lived.
On his way, the soldier fell in with an
old woman and having a kindly
heart, carried her bundles as he
walked along beside her.

'What are you seeking in the big
city?' the old woman asked him by
way of conversation.

'Why, that I can hardly say, old
mother,' said the soldier smiling. 'But
life holds little promise for a limping
soldier, that I do know!'

'Do not be too certain of that,' said
the old woman. 'Who knows what
glory may lie in wait for you?'

The soldier laughed heartily at the
very idea. 'Why, what shall I do, old
mother?' he teased. 'Shall I find out

how the princesses dance through their shoes, and so become king of all this fine land?' He spoke in jest, but the old woman answered him in earnest.

'That is possible,' she said, 'if you will only remember not to drink the wine they give you.'

'You speak as if you know something of their secrets,' said the soldier. 'Yet how should I see their revels without being seen myself?'

'Give me your warm cloak,' said the old woman, 'and I will give you mine. With it you may pass unseen, and yet may watch them as you will.'

The soldier gave her his warm cloak and took hers, which seemed light and shadowy. When he wrapped it around him, he found to his astonishment that she told the truth. Looking down at his feet, he could see only a clump of grass and the stones of the road. He took the cloak off quickly and was relieved to see his worn boots reappear.

'Why, bless you, old mother,' he said. 'If I become king, you shall want for nothing.' And with that he set off for the palace to try his fortune.

The king was a little put out to find a common, bearded soldier, with patched clothes and worn boots, presenting himself as a suitor for one of the princesses. But he was a man of his word, and gave orders that the soldier was to be treated as courteously as the other suitors. He was given a bath in the royal bathroom, fine clothes, and a good meal before the night came. Then he was led with honour into a small antechamber next to the princesses' bedroom. The outer doors were bolted and the inner doors left open, so that

the princesses could not leave unseen
by any other way.

As the weary soldier settled himself
into the comfortable chair set ready
for him, the eldest princess came
through from the bedroom bearing a
goblet of wine in her slender hands.
She smiled and said, 'Will you drink
with us, soldier, to show that you bear
us no ill will?'

The soldier took the cup, feeling
that it would be churlish to refuse her.
But he had not forgotten the old
woman's warning and, while taking
his bath, he had hidden the royal
bath-sponge under his chin, behind his
beard. He lifted the cup to his lips and
seemed to be drinking it, but all the
time, the wine trickled down unseen
through his beard, and soaked into
the sponge. He thought the eldest
princess looked a little sorry as she

took away the empty cup. He leaned back, yawned, closed his eyes and began to snore.

A distant voice called, 'Is he sleeping?'

'He is, indeed,' answered the eldest princess, but it seemed to the soldier that she sighed as she said it.

The eldest princess went back into the great bedroom and, at once, the soldier put down the sponge full of wine, and threw the shadowy cloak about him. As he passed unseen into the princesses' bedroom, he found that they were all putting on their dancing dresses, and fitting their dainty feet into shiny new shoes. They were laughing and chattering and eager for the dance, all except the youngest who said: 'I have a strange feeling that all is not well tonight.'

'Silly goose!' said the eldest. 'It will

be as it has always been. The soldier
sleeps as soundly as the princes who
came before him.' Then she tapped
three times upon the end of her gilded
bed, and at once it sank down into
the floor. The eldest princess stepped
down into the opening and one by
one her sisters followed her. And
behind the youngest came the soldier,
walking upon tiptoe though none
could see him. Down beneath the
earth led the flight of steps and as the
soldier limped behind, he trod by
accident upon the youngest princess's
dress.

She cried out and turned in alarm,
but seeing no-one, said only, 'It
seemed that someone caught at my
dress!'

'Silly goose!' called her eldest sister.
'You must have caught it upon a
nail!'

At the bottom of the flight of steps stood a wide avenue of shimmering silver trees. As they passed along it, the soldier broke off a twig and hid it under his cloak. Hearing the twig snap, the youngest princess cried out again. But the eldest said: 'It is only our princes firing salutes to welcome us.'

They came next to an avenue where the trees glittered with leaves of gold, and then to another which sparkled with diamonds. Each time the soldier snapped off a twig and the youngest princess took fright. But each time the eldest laughed and said she was a goose, for the shots were fired to welcome them.

At the end of the avenues, a wide lake spread before them. Beyond it stood a splendid palace shining with light, and alive with the sound of music. Twelve boats stood by the shore, each with a bright lantern on the prow, and twelve princes waited at the oars. Each prince took one of the princesses and ferried her across the lake. The soldier scrambled in behind the youngest princess.

'How heavy the boat seems tonight,' said the prince who was rowing it.

When they reached the shining palace, the dancing began. Each princess danced with her prince and the soldier passed unseen amidst them all. Once, as the eldest princess held a goblet of wine, the soldier drank from it, so that when she raised it to her lips she found it empty. But the eldest princess only laughed and filled it again.

Hour after hour, the twelve princesses danced and would not rest until their shoes were all in holes. Then at last, their princes rowed them back across the shining lake and, this time, the soldier took his place beside the eldest. Gently he touched her hand, but she took it for the fluttering of a moth about the boat's lantern.

When they reached the far shore, the twelve princesses took leave of their princes and hurried back through the glistening trees. This time the soldier ran ahead and by the time the princesses reached their bedroom, he was snoring peacefully in his chair.

'Poor man,' said the eldest princess sadly, as she thought of the soldier's fate.

When the king came in the

morning, the soldier said nothing of what he had seen. He had resolved to watch the princesses through the three nights allowed to him, so that he might know them better and make his choice wisely. The second and third nights passed like the first: again, the twelve princesses danced their shoes to pieces. And each night the soldier watched the eldest princess and saw that she was bold and fearless, a fit wife for a soldier. On the third night the soldier brought back a golden goblet as proof of what had passed.

When the time came for the soldier to answer or die, he wrapped the twigs and the goblet in the magic cloak. He heard the princesses whispering together as the guards led him into the king's presence.

'Now, soldier,' said the king when all were assembled. 'If you are to

save your life you must tell me
where it is that my daughters dance
all night, wearing their shoes into
pieces.'

'Why, my Lord,' said the soldier,
'they dance beneath the ground in a
splendid palace beyond a shining
lake,' and he told his story just as it
had happened.

'You tell a strange tale,' said the
king thoughtfully. 'Perchance it is no
more than a fairy story told to save
your own neck.'

Then the soldier removed the cloak
and presented to the king the three
twigs and the golden goblet. When
the king saw them he called his
daughters to stand before him, and
asked them if the soldier spoke the
truth. The younger princesses
mumbled and hesitated and, casting
their eyes down, were at a loss how to

answer him. But the eldest smiled and spoke out boldly, 'It is true, Father,' she said, 'and this brave soldier has the better of us!'

Then the king turned again to the soldier and bade him choose a bride among his daughters.

Now, the soldier had come to love the eldest princess, but he was a plain man and love made him shy. He could not speak what he felt, but only said: 'Your Majesty, I am past my first youth so I will take the eldest one.'

The eldest princess laughed: she heard his words, but she also saw his shyness. 'A pretty compliment, indeed!' she said. 'But the soldier will suit me well, Father.'

The princess and her soldier were married that same day and lived in great contentment together. And when, in time, they came to rule that land, they did so with courage and wisdom and good humour.

This is a story by the Brothers Grimm, re-told by Antonia Barber.

The Werewolf Knight

Feolf was a knight and a good friend
of the king, but at other times he was
a werewolf. That is to say, when the
moon rose over the tops of the pine
trees, Sir Feolf took off his fine
woollen tunic and his cloak, hid them
under a big rock, and turned into a
wolf. All night long he would run in
the forest, and when morning came
he would change into a man again,
get dressed and go home, and no-one
was any the wiser.

Now a werewolf is a horrible beast
to see, with his long fangs and his red

tongue and his smoking breath, and Feolf was careful that no-one ever saw him in this state; for even as a wolf his heart was kind, and he did not want to frighten anyone.

And so it was that the Lady Fioran, who was Feolf's dearest friend, walked with him in the garden, and sat with him at dinner, and never once suspected there was anything amiss.

Fioran was the daughter of the king, and loved Feolf even more than her father did. When the king saw this he was greatly pleased, for Feolf and Fioran were the two he loved best in all the world. And when Feolf and Fioran decided to get married, the king was overjoyed.

The king called for a feast that night, to mark the great event. The cups were filled with mead, the lords and ladies chattered, and the minstrels sang of great deeds long ago.

But before their song was ended, the moon rose. And Feolf slipped away to the forest and turned into a wolf.

He did not come back till morning, and then Fioran found him walking in the garden. 'Where have you been, Feolf?' she asked.

But Feolf would not answer.

Then Fioran began to weep, for she was afraid he no longer loved her; and when Feolf saw this he was sorry, and told her his secret.

Fioran was deeply troubled. She loved the knight very much, but it is a different thing to be married to a werewolf, and to tell the truth she was very much afraid. She imagined the wolf, with his gleaming eyes and his cruel teeth and his lolling tongue, and she dreaded marrying such a horrible beast.

And so she puzzled and grew more sad, and the wedding day drew closer and closer.

On the eve of her wedding day she went to the court magician and asked him what she should do.

'The answer is simple,' said the magician, who would have liked to marry Fioran himself. 'When Sir Feolf goes to the forest tonight he will hide his clothes under a rock. You must bring back his clothes and give them to me.'

'Is that all?' said Fioran. 'Just bring back his clothes?'

'Then all will be well,' said the magician.

That night, when Feolf slipped away to the forest, Fioran followed him. She brought back his clothes just as she was told and gave them to the magician.

When Feolf saw that his clothes were gone he pawed the ground and searched, and snuffed, and howled most piteously. 'Fioran!' he cried. 'Fioran!'

But a wolf does not have the gift of human speech, and only the crows in the pine trees heard him, and flapped their wings.

And so it was that Feolf did not come back to the castle that morning. For without his clothes he could not change back into human form, but must stay for ever a wolf.

Far away in the castle, on her wedding day, Fioran waited. She put on her wedding dress and twined flowers in her hair, but Feolf did not come.

In the evening she went to the court

magician. 'Where is he?' she asked. 'What has happened to him?'

'He was a werewolf,' said the magician. 'You are better off without him.'

Then Fioran shut herself in her room and wept for her lost knight, and no-one could comfort her; not the ladies of the court, nor the jesters, and not even the court magician, who kept sending her little presents.

The king was deeply saddened at the loss of his favourite knight, and decreed a time of mourning. There was no more feasting and no more dancing, and the minstrels hung their lutes on the wall.

Summer passed and autumn came, and Feolf stayed in the forest, living on wild roots and pine needles. The days grew colder and darker, and Feolf longed to be in the castle once again. He missed the feasting and the dancing, and he missed the warmth of his feather bed. But he missed Fioran most of all.

The king's sorrow grew as winter came, and one day his courtiers, trying to distract him, persuaded him to go hunting with them in the forest. 'We might kill a bear,' they said. 'Or a wolf.'

And so one icy day the king rode out with his huntsmen and his hounds. Feolf heard the hunting horns from far off and laughed for joy, for he knew the king was coming; and he ran to meet his master, loping his wolfish lope and grinning his wolfish grin.

The huntsmen saw the wolf as he came on them in the clearing, but they did not know it was Feolf. They saw the horrible beast with his dripping jaws and his glittering eyes, and the nearest huntsman aimed his spear.

'Stop!' cried the king. 'Drop your spear!'

The huntsman dropped his spear, but he kept his eye on the wolf. 'Take care, sire,' he said. 'A wolf is a savage beast, and should be killed before it does harm.'

But the king looked long at Feolf, and said, 'He is a sad wolf, and I cannot find it in my heart to kill him. Take him back to the castle and give him food and find him a warm place to sleep.'

The huntsmen thought the king's long grief had turned his mind, and some would have killed the wolf then and there if they had not feared the king's anger. But they tied a rope round Feolf's neck, keeping well clear of his jaws, and started off for the castle.

When they drew near the castle Feolf lifted his head and sniffed; and then he bayed and howled with joy.

Fioran in her bedchamber heard it, and came running out in her dressing-gown, and ran to meet him and kissed him, and held his shaggy head between her hands and wept. Those who saw it were amazed, and all agreed that he was a very gentle wolf, even a noble wolf, but no-one could tell the reason.

Fioran called the court magician and told him to bring Feolf's clothes. And before the astonished court Feolf put his clothes on and stood there once more as a noble knight.

The king was overjoyed to see Feolf again, the more so because Feolf had been loyal to him twice over; for even as a wolf he had been true to his king.

Then the king caused a feast to be set in the great hall, with dancing and merriment. The lutes were tuned again, the minstrels smoothed their throats with ale, and the ladies got out their dancing shoes.

Feolf and Fioran led the dancing that night, and when the moon rose Feolf did not go to the forest, but stayed with his bride. He had had enough of running wild in the forest, and from now on he was content to be just a man.

Only sometimes, when the night was particularly cold or the moon particularly bright, Feolf would slip

away to the forest. But then Fioran
kept a spare set of clothes for him, just
in case.

This story is by Jenny Wagner.

Lizzie Dripping by Moonlight

Lizzie Dripping often felt a prickle at the back of her neck when she read a poem she liked. It was rather like the prickle she felt whenever she went tiptoe and breath-held into the graveyard to see if the witch was there – *her* witch. Not exactly the same, because with a poem it was a prickle of delight. With the witch it was fright and delight.

Although Lizzie thought of her as *her* witch, and a friend of sorts, she was a tricky customer. She came and went as she pleased, refused to tell her

name and was quite capable of
turning cats into toads.

★   ★   ★

Slowly, silently, now the moon
Walks the night in her silver shoon;
This way, and that, she peers, and sees
Silver fruit upon silver trees.

Lizzie, who up till now had been
daydreaming, as usual, felt that
delicious, slow tingle along her spine.
Her teacher was a good reader, and
she picked good poems. Lizzie listened
spellbound and the tingle was still
there when the poem ended.

A harvest mouse goes scampering by,
With silver claws and silver eye;
And moveless fish in the water gleam,
By silver reeds in a silver stream.

Miss Platt's voice stopped. Lizzie

waited. Surely there was more? She wanted the poem to go on and on.

'Is that all?' she asked. The rest of the class tittered and Lizzie felt her face fire.

'I'm afraid so,' said Miss Platt. 'Though you could always try writing another verse of your own.' So she could, thought Lizzie Dripping. And she might, at that. But what she already longed for was to see a silver world of her own.

Was it *really* silver, at night, under the moon? Did trees, hedges, field and farm gleam and shine as if brushed with frost? Would the cows have silver eyes, and the sheep? Best of all, would she *herself* be silver?

At dinner time she asked Patty, her mother.

'Mam, does the world really go silver at night?'

'What?' Patty was dishing out the shepherd's pie, and only half listening, as usual. 'Does the what?'

'World go silver. At night. When there's a moon, I mean.'

'That's just your daft kind of question, Lizzie Dripping,' her mother told her.

'Bit difficult to tell, these days,' said Albert, her father. 'It's the street lights, see. Neither moon nor stars, when there's street lights. But in the old days . . . aye . . . I reckon it *was* kind of silvery.'

'Then you've different eyes from *mine*,' Patty told him. 'Silver!'

And just then Toby set up yelling, and that was the end of that. It was the end of the conversation, at any rate. But Lizzie Dripping went on thinking, and what she wondered now was whether the moon was full.

That night, after Patty had gone back downstairs, Lizzie climbed out of bed and drew back the curtain. She could see the dark shape of the church tower and the sheep under the apple trees in the field opposite. The street lamps were orangey when you looked at them, but they didn't give a golden light. Lizzie's gaze travelled upwards and – her breath caught in her throat – the moon! It was there, full and round and white, hanging above the roof of Bell Brigg farm. Lizzie's spine dissolved into a long, slow tingle.

'Tomorrow,' she thought. 'Tomorrow night!' Because Lizzie Dripping had already decided that if there *were* a silver world out there, she was going to discover it. 'I'd have to go out the village,' she thought, as she lay plotting her plot. 'In the fields, where there's no light.' The thought

was a little frightening, though she didn't see why.

'There'll only be sheep and cows,' she thought, 'and mice and that, with silver claws and silver eye.' Then, 'the witch!'

That was a very different kettle of fish. If Lizzie was to go walking out of Little Hemlock alone, at night, then the last thing she wanted to know was that the witch was about. A witch in broad daylight and only a stone's throw away from home was one thing. A witch at night, by moonlight, was definitely another. There was only one thing to do.

Next day was Saturday. Lizzie, as usual, was sent up to the shop, and as usual was told to give Toby a push.

'Does he *have* to go?' Lizzie was going to call at the graveyard, as well as the shop. 'I think he's bored with being pushed up to the shop.'

'Of course he ain't, are you, my lamb?' Patty lifted Toby and plonked him in his pushchair.

'You're a nuisance,' Lizzie told him as she pushed him down the path. 'Toby Arbuckle's a great fat nuisance, Toby Arbuckle's a great fat nuisance!' Toby gurgled plumply and waved his knitted cat by the tail.

'Well, don't blame *me* if you get turned toad!' Lizzie told him. A while back, she had seen with her own eyes the Briggs' black-and-white tom turned into a toad. Luckily, the witch had been in a good mood that day, and had turned him back again.

'If that witch turns *Toby* into a toad, I'll never be able to go back home again,' thought Lizzie Dripping. 'Not ever.'

Up at the shop she bought the

things for her mother and then spent part of her pocket money on sweets for Toby. 'To keep him quiet,' she thought. 'Then I'll push him into the church porch, where the witch can't see him.'

Though she could not be sure, not absolutely sure, that the witch *wouldn't* see him. For all she knew, that witch could see through stone. She reached the church and pushed Toby by the steep, grassy bank that she always thought of as a pathway into the sky. When she reached the little wrought iron gate at the top she stopped and listened. Only the whistle of birds, the soft sough of the wind in the seeding grasses, the bleat of lambs from the home field. Lizzie took a deep breath and went through the gate. She wheeled Toby into the porch, then gave him the sweets.

'You stop here, Toby,' she told him. 'Lizzie'll be back soon.' As she turned the corner of the church her eyes went straight to the wide flat tomb of 'Hannah Post of this parish' and 'Albert Cyril, beloved husband of the above 1802–1879. Peace, Perfect Peace.' That was where the witch would sit, endlessly knitting in black wool what looked like a shawl for a witch baby. Not there!

Lizzie was not surprised. The witch could make herself visible or invisible in the blink of an eye. And she liked playing hide-and-seek. Lizzie called softly.

'Witch? Witch, where are you?' No reply. Not even the twitch of a grass by the tomb of the Perfectly Peaceful Posts. 'It's me! Lizzie!' Silence. Then – Lizzie stiffened – a thin, high cackle from somewhere near, somewhere behind her. Round she whirled. Nothing. Not a sign.

'Knit one, purl one, slip one, knit one, pass the slip stitch over . . .'

Slowly, breath held, Lizzie turned again. There she sat, her witch, hunched over her tattered knitting. 'I spy with my little eye!' The witch did not even look up.

'Oh witch! You *are* there!' Lizzie edged closer, but not too close. 'It looks smashing. Your knitting, I mean.'

'S'all right,' said the witch. 'What d'you want?'

'Oh! Oh, nothing,' Lizzie lied. 'Just wanted to see you, that's all.'

The witch did look at her now, with her fierce bright eyes. It was as if she could see right through Lizzie – read her thoughts, even. Lizzie swallowed hard.

'Witch . . .'

'Well? What is it, girl?'

'I wondered . . . I mean, when I come to see you, it's always daytime, see. What I wondered . . . is . . . do you come at night, as well?'

'Day, night, sun, moon – 's'all the same to me!' The witch's black-mittened hands were working her needles again.

'So – you do come out at night?'

'Maybe do – maybe don't!' said the witch unhelpfully. Click click went the wooden needles. Lizzie decided to try another tack.

'Witch – there's a full moon. When there is . . . is . . . does the world turn silver?' The witch stuck her pins into the ball of wool and thrust her knitting deep into the black folds of her cloak. She sat then, musing, rocking a little from side to side. And when she did speak, it was in a dreamy, singsong way, as if to herself. 'Moonlight . . . owl light . . . bat light . . .' she crooned, '*witch* light . . .'

'Oh dear,' thought poor Lizzie Dripping. 'She *does* come out at night.'

'Bats fly, owls hoots, witches ride . . . and the moon's huge and white, and the whole world's . . .' she paused.

'Yes?' prompted Lizzie softly, hardly daring, 'Yes?'

'Silver . . .' The witch whispered the word, stroked it, as if it were a cat. 'Silver!'

'Ah . . .' Lizzie let out a long held breath. So the witch did inhabit the world of the night and the witch saw a world of silver at every full moon. 'Oh,' she said, and now she too was speaking her thoughts aloud. 'Oh, I'd give anything to see it, anything!'

'Then see it, girl, see it!' the witch snapped. She was back to her usual self again now, tart and crabby.

'But I can't! I mean . . . I mean . . .'

'Daren't?' suggested the witch slyly, tilting her head. 'Daren't — because of me?'

'Yes. No . . . oh, I don't know!' Lizzie was almost in tears now.

'But *I* know.' The witch looked at her now, very long and hard. '*I* know . . .' And as she spoke, she vanished. She did not vanish in a twinkling, as she usually did. She faded, dissolved into the green air by the hedge. Lizzie strained into the shadows, but there was not the least hint that the witch might still be there, even invisibly there.

'Witch?' she called. 'Witch?' She

wheeled about, scanning the leaning, barnacled tombstones, the knee-high grass and wind-bent trees. The world was suddenly empty and bleak, as it always was after the witch vanished.

'But she's there somewhere,' Lizzie comforted herself. 'Must be. Invisibly there.'

Then she remembered Toby, and found him smothered in chocolate in the church porch. He beamed, a sticky beam.

'Look at you! Just look at you!' The smile faded. The round blue eyes fixed anxiously on Lizzie's. In a flash she was contrite. She had spoilt his morning just as the witch had spoilt hers.

'Oh Toby! 'S'not your fault! Come on, sausage – Lizzie loves you!' And she swept him up from his chair, chocolate and all, and hugged him.

And even as she did so she knew that it was as much to comfort herself as him.

The rest of the day, the long stretch that lay between sun and moonlight, was long and unsatisfactory. Lizzie loved Saturdays, as a rule. She dawdled and dreamed her way through them as sleek and happy as a cat – if Patty let her. Today, she could settle to nothing. The world itself seemed drained of colour, drab and dull. Lizzie's thoughts were fixed on another world entirely – a silver one. She felt that she would die if she couldn't see it. To relieve her feelings, she *did* write another verse to the poem Miss Platt had read:

> *I walk the night down the quiet lane*
> *White and shining as if with rain,*

Down to the fields where lie in peace
Silvery sheep with their silver fleece.

She was quite pleased with it, in a
way. 'Only thing is, it's a cheat,' she
thought. 'I haven't been down the
lane at night, nor seen silvery sheep.'
What was worse, she couldn't be sure
that she ever would. For all she knew,
she had that witch for life. And now
she knew for a fact that the witch
came out at night.

She would be there, lurking in the
spiky shadows, brimming with spells.
And Lizzie Dripping felt in her bones
that night spells were dangerous, not
to be sneezed at.

'Dare I?' she wondered. 'Or daren't
I?' She never gave a thought to Patty,
and what she would say if she found
that Lizzie was up and out by night,

walking the fields alone in the moonlight.

'Easy enough to slip out,' she thought. 'They'll be watching the telly and never notice.' Even if, by some stroke of ill luck, Patty did find out, it was not the end of the world. But if, out there in the wide, moon-bleached fields, she met a witch – that might be the end of the world.

It went on all day. 'Dare I . . . daren't I? Dare I . . . daren't I?' In the end, she didn't have to decide. It was at teatime when the blow fell. 'Lucky Blod was free,' Lizzie heard her mother say, 'else we couldn't've gone.'

'Gone where?' demanded Lizzie.

'Whist Drive, tonight, at the village hall. Your Aunt Blodwen's coming to baby-sit.'

'Oh no!' It was one thing to get

past Patty and Albert, another thing entirely to get past Aunt Blod, with her sharp Welsh eyes and sharp Welsh ears. Lizzie's beautiful world of silver splintered like glass before her eyes. 'Now I'll never see it,' she thought. 'Never. Not till the next full moon, anyhow.' But the next full moon was light years away, an eternity. 'I'll die,' thought Lizzie Dripping. 'I'll just die.' She told herself this quite often.

At just before seven Aunt Blod arrived with her knitting, and Albert and Patty went off.

'Bed at eight, mind, Lizzie,' Patty called as she went.

'I'll see to it, Patty,' Blod said. 'Don't believe in children up all hours, watching telly and ruining their eyes.' The back door shut.

'I don't watch telly,' Lizzie told her coldly. 'I read.'

'Ruin your eyes just as easy reading,' said Aunt Blod smugly. 'Eight o'clock, Lizzie, and not a moment after.' In the end, Lizzie went to bed early. Better to lie in bed reading than stop with Aunt Blod and the click click click of her needles.

'Nearly dark!' Lizzie peered through the curtains. The moon was already hanging there, but pale and washed out. The street lamps glowed orange and she could see the lights of the village hall by the church.

'If ever I'm prime minister,' she told herself savagely, 'there'll be a law against street lamps!' She dropped the curtain and climbed into bed. She had a good book – one about a boy who was snatched away by an eagle – but she could not keep her mind on it. All the time, mixed in with pictures of the soaring eagle, were other pictures of a world in the moonlight, a silver world.

After about an hour she gave a sigh and looked at the clock on her bedside table. Nearly nine o'clock. 'Dark outside, now,' she thought. 'At least, dark except for the moonlight. Just finish this chapter and – oh!'

The light went out. At the very same moment the music and laughter from below, where Aunt Blod was watching television, stopped dead. For a moment there was darkness and silence. Then a shriek from Aunt Blodwen.

'Electricity cut,' thought Lizzie. They had them, from time to time, and Patty always had candles ready. She could hear Aunt Blod stumbling about below, looking for them. Lizzie lay there, and as she did so became aware that the room was no longer dark. Her eyes went to the curtains – the pattern was showing, as it did first thing in the morning.

'The moon!' Lizzie was out of bed and at the window and then staring out at a new world. She had known the scene all her life, but now it lay foreign, strangely other under a broad, white light. The street lamp had been snuffed out like a candle and the moon had come into its own. Each apple tree in the orchard below was dappled silver and stood anchored in a sharp black shadow. The grass was bleached as if thick with hoar frost. Here and there lay the sheep. 'Silvery sheep with their silver fleece! 'S'true, then! The world *does* turn silver!'

Down below Aunt Blodwen was

muttering to herself, still searching for candles. Lizzie did not even hear her. She was gazing out at a world that till now she had hardly dreamed of, and thinking what a miracle it was that all the lights should go out tonight, of all nights. A miracle, or – the witch!

Was she out there, stalking the silver night, rubbing her skinny palms with glee. Could a witch make the lights go out?

Lizzie Dripping leaned right out of the open window and the moon shone full on her face and she could have sworn that she actually felt herself turn silver.

'Witch?' she called softly. 'Witch! Thank you, witch!'

An owl hooted mournfully from the beeches down below. There was a sudden screech – which might have been that of a moorhen by the lake, frightened by a fox. Or might have been that of a witch . . . a silver witch?

This story is by Helen Cresswell.

The Sea-Baby

The stocking-basket was empty. For once there was nothing to darn. The Old Nurse had told so many stories, that she had mended all the holes made by Doris and Mary Matilda, and even by Ronnie and Roley. Tomorrow they would make some more, of course, but tonight the Old Nurse sat with her hands folded in her lap, and watched the children fall asleep by fire-light.

Only one of them kept awake. Mary Matilda would not go to sleep. She was not cross, she was not ill, there was no reason at all except that she was wide awake. She kept on standing up in her cot and laughing at the Old Nurse over the bars. And when the Old Nurse came and laid her down and tucked her up, she turned over and laughed at the Old Nurse *between* the cot-bars.

'Go to sleep, Mary Matilda,' said the Old Nurse in her hush-hush voice. 'Shut your eyes, my darling, and go to sleep.'

But Mary Matilda couldn't, or if she could, she wouldn't. And at last the Old Nurse did what she very seldom did: she came over to Mary Matilda, and took her out of the cot, and carried her to the fire, and rocked her on her knee.

'Can't you go to sleep, baby?' she crooned. 'Can't you go to sleep, then? Ah, you're just my Sea-Baby over

123

again! *She* never went to sleep, either, all the time I nursed her. And she was the very first I ever nursed. I've never told anybody about her since, but I'll tell you, Mary Matilda. So shut your eyes and listen, while I tell about my Sea-Baby.

I couldn't tell you when it happened: it was certainly a long time after the Flood, and I know I was only about ten years old, and had never left the Norfolk village on the sea-coast where I was born. My father was a fisherman, and a tiller of the land; and my mother kept the house and spun the wool and linen for our clothes. But that tells us nothing, for fathers have provided the food, and mothers have kept the house, since the beginning of things. So don't go asking any more when it was that

I nursed my very first baby.

It happened like this, Mary Matilda. Our cottage stood near the edge of the cliff, and at high tide the sea came right up to the foot, but at low tide it ran so far back that it seemed almost too far to follow it. People said that once, long ago, the sea had not come in so close; and that the cliff had gone out many miles farther. And on the far end of the cliff had stood another village. But after the Flood all that part of the cliff was drowned under the sea, and the village along with it. And there, said the people, the village still lay, far out to sea under the waves; and on stormy nights, they said, you could hear the church bells ringing in the church tower below the water. Ah, don't you start laughing at your old Nanny now! We knew it was true, I tell you. And one day something happened to prove it.

A big storm blew up over our part of the land; the biggest storm that any of us could remember, so big that we thought the Flood had come again. The sky was as black as night all day long, and the wind blew so hard that it drove a strong man backwards, and the rain poured down so that you only had to hold a pitcher out of the window for a second, and when you took it in it was flowing over, and the thunder growled and crackled so that we had to make signs to each other, for talking was no use, and the lightning flashed so bright that my mother could thread her needle by it. That *was* a storm, that was! My mother was frightened, but my father, who was weather-wise, watched the sky and said from time to time, 'I

think that'll come out all right.' And
so it did. The lightning and thunder
flashed and rolled themselves away
into the distance, the rain stopped, the
wind died down, the sky cleared up
for a beautiful evening, and the sun
turned all the vast wet sands to a
sheet of gold as far as the eye could
see. Yes, and farther! For a wonder
had happened during the storm. The
sea had been driven back so far that it
had vanished out of sight, and sands
were laid bare that no living man or
woman had viewed before. And there,
far, far across the golden beach, lay a
tiny village, shining in the setting sun.

Think of our excitement, Mary
Matilda! It was the drowned village of
long ago, come back to the light of
day.

Everybody gathered on the shore to
look at it. And suddenly I began to

run towards it, and all the other children followed me. At first our parents called, 'Come back! Come back! The sea may come rolling in before you can get there.' But we were too eager to see the village for ourselves, and in the end the big folk felt the same about it; and they came running after the children across the sands. As we drew nearer, the little houses became plainer, looking like blocks of gold in the evening light; and the little streets appeared like golden brooks, and the church spire in the middle was like a point of fire.

For all my little legs, I was the first to reach the village. I had had a start of the others, and could always run fast as a child and never tire. We had long stopped running, of course, for the village was so far out that our breath would not last. But I was still

walking rapidly when I reached the
village and turned a corner. As I did
so, I heard one of the big folk cry,
'Oh, look! Yonder lies the sea.' I
glanced ahead, and did see, on the far
horizon beyond the village, the
shining line of the sea that had gone
so far away. Then I heard another
grown-up cry, 'Take care! Take care!
Who knows when it may begin to roll
back again? We have come far, and
oh, suppose the sea should overtake us
before we can reach home!' Then,
peeping round my corner, I saw
everybody take fright and turn tail,
running as hard as they could across
the mile or so of sands they had just
crossed. But nobody had noticed me,
or thought of me; no doubt my own
parents thought I was one of the
band of running children, and so
they left me alone there, with all

the little village to myself.

What a lovely time I had, going into the houses, up and down the streets, and through the church. Everything was left as it had been, and seemed ready for someone to come to; the flowers were blooming in the gardens, the fruit was hanging on the trees, the tables were spread for the next meal, a pot was standing by the kettle on the hearth in one house, and in another there were toys upon the floor. And when I began to go upstairs to the other rooms, I found in every bed someone asleep. Grandmothers and grandfathers, mothers and fathers, young men and young women, boys and girls: all so fast asleep, that there was no waking them. And at last, in a little room at the top of a house, I found a baby in a cradle, wide awake.

She was the sweetest baby I had ever seen. Her eyes were as blue as the sea that had covered them so long, her skin as white as the foam, and her little round head as gold as the sands in the evening sunlight. When she saw me, she sat up in her cradle, and crowed with delight. I knelt down beside her, held out my arms, and she cuddled into them with a little gleeful chuckle. I carried her about the room, dancing her up and down in my arms, calling her my baby, my pretty Sea-Baby, and showing her the things in the room and out of the window. But as we were looking out of the window at a bird's nest in a tree, I seemed to see the shining line of water on the horizon begin to move.

'The sea is coming in!' I thought. 'I must hurry back before it catches us.'

And I flew out of the house with the Sea-Baby in my arms, and ran as fast as I could out of the village, and followed the crowd of golden footsteps on the sands, anxious to get home soon. When I had to pause to get my breath, I ventured to glance over my shoulder, and there behind me lay the little village, still glinting in the sun. On I ran again, and after a while was forced to stop a second time. Once more I glanced behind me, and this time the village was not to be seen: it had disappeared beneath the tide of the sea, which was rolling in behind me.

Then how I scampered over the rest of the way! I reached home just as the tiny wavelets, which run in front of the big waves, began to lap my ankles, and I scrambled up the cliff, with the Sea-Baby in my arms, and got indoors, panting for breath. Nobody was at home, for as it happened they were all out looking for me. So I took my baby upstairs, and put her to bed in my own bed, and got her some warm milk. But she turned from the milk, and wouldn't drink it. She only seemed to want to laugh and play with me. So I did for a little while, and then I told her she must go to sleep. But she only laughed some more, and went on playing.

'Shut your eyes, baby,' I said to her, 'hush–hush! Hush–hush!' (just as my own mother said to me). But the baby didn't seem to understand, and went on laughing.

Then I said, 'You're a very naughty baby' (as my mother sometimes used to say to me). But she didn't mind that either, and just went on laughing. So in the end I had to laugh too, and play with her.

My mother heard us, when she came into the house; and she ran up to find me, delighted that I was safe. What was her surprise to find the baby with me! She asked me where it had come from, and I told her; and she called my father, and he stood scratching his head, as most men do when they aren't quite sure about a thing.

'I want to keep it for my own, Mother,' I said.

'Well, we can't turn it out now it's in,' said my mother. 'But you'll have to look after it yourself, mind.'

I wanted nothing better! I'd always wanted to nurse things, whether it was a log of wood, or a kitten, or my mother's shawl rolled into a dumpy bundle. And now I had a little live baby of my own to nurse. How I did enjoy myself that week! I did everything for it; dressed and undressed it, washed it, and combed its hair; and played and danced with it, and talked with it and walked with it. And I tried to give it its meals, but it wouldn't eat; and I tried to put it to sleep, but it wouldn't shut its eyes. No, not for anything I could do, though I sang to it, and rocked it, and told it little stories.

It didn't worry me much, for I knew no better: but it worried my mother, and I heard her say to my father, 'There's something queer about that child. I don't know, I'm sure!'

On the seventh night after the storm, I woke up suddenly from my dreams, as I lay in bed with my baby beside me. It was very late, my parents had long gone to bed

themselves, and what had wakened
me I did not know, for I heard no
sound at all. The moon was very
bright, and filled the square of my
window-pane with silver light; and
through the air outside I saw
something swimming – I thought at
first it was a white cloud, but as it
reached my open window I saw it
was a lady, moving along the air as
though she were swimming in water.
And the strange thing was that her
eyes were fast shut; so that as her
white arms moved out and in she
seemed to be swimming not only in
the air, but in her sleep.

She swam straight through my
open window to the bedside, and
there she came to rest, letting her feet
down upon the floor like a swimmer
setting his feet on the sands under his
body. The lady leaned over the bed

with her eyes shut, and took my wide-awake baby in her arms.

'*Hush-hush! Hush-hush!*' she said; and the sound of her voice was not like my mother's voice when she said it, but like the waves washing the shore on a still night; such a peaceful sound, the sort of sound that might have been the first sound made in the world, or else the last. You couldn't help wanting to sleep as you heard her say it. I felt my head begin to nod, and as it grew heavier and heavier, I noticed that my Sea-Baby's eyelids were beginning to droop too. Before I could see any more, I fell asleep; and when I awoke in the morning my baby had gone.

'Where to, Mary Matilda? Ah, you mustn't ask me that! I only know she must have gone where all babies go

when they go to sleep. Go to sleep.
Hush-hush! *Hush-hush! Go to sleep!'*

Mary Matilda had gone to sleep at
last. The Old Nurse laid her softly in
her cot, turned down the light, and
crept out of the nursery.

This story is by Eleanor Farjeon.

How the Moon Began

This is the story of how the moon began. Once upon a time there was no moon. The nights were as black as black. If you went out without a lantern, ten to one you bumped into somebody else. So people gave up going out at night and stayed at home. Usually they went to bed as soon as the sun disappeared behind the mountains.

Now there was no blacker place at night than the land of Exe. One fine morning, bright and early, four men of Exe set out to do business in the

land of Wye. They were brothers.
The first one's name was Arn, which
means 'the old one'.

The second one's name was Bor,
which means 'the quiet one'.

The third one's name was Cass,
which means 'a man of deeds'; and
the fourth one's name was Deol,
which means 'cunning' or 'crafty'.

When the four men of Exe had
done their business in Wye, they
started for home. Soon the sun went
down, and night overtook them. But
the night was not dark, as in their
own country. Nor was it as bright as
day. It was half-and-half – light
enough for the four men to see each
other and to see their way.

''Tis a very bright night for the
time of day,' said Arn. 'Very different
from home. What be the cause of it,
Brother Bor?'

Bor said nothing, but Cass said, 'There is a light over there, right above yonder oak tree.'

'That is a very clever contraption,' Deol said, nodding his head wisely.

'Aye, that it is,' Arn said. 'What can it be, I wonder?'

In the soft light that shone all round them they saw a man of Wye approaching.

They stopped him, and Cass said, 'What is that light, sir? It seems to be a very good light.'

'Ah,' replied the man of Wye, 'that is the moon. Our Mayor bought it for two pounds ten and hung it up over that oak tree. It lights up the whole country. We have to pay him six and eightpence a week to fill it with oil and keep it clean, so that it burns steady all night.'

'Thank you, sir,' said Deol, 'and goodnight to you.'

'Let us take this moon,' said Arn. 'The people of Wye can very well buy another one for themselves, and this is exactly what we need back home. We have an oak tree just as good as this one, and there we will hang it to enlighten the whole of Exe.'

'You are right, Brother Arn,' Cass said. 'You and Deol go and find a cart, while Brother Bor climbs into the tree to fetch this moon down. Brother Bor is just the man to climb to the top of the tree.'

So Arn and Deol went to fetch a cart, while Bor clambered into the tree, cut a hole in the lamp and passed a rope through it.

He and Cass lowered it to the

ground, and together the four brothers lifted it into the cart. Then they covered the shining ball with their cloaks so that no-one could see what they had stolen. With two of them in front of the cart and two at the back, they pushed it home to the land of Exe.

They hung it on the top of a tall oak tree, and everyone in Exe was delighted with their new lamp. The soft light shone into sitting rooms and bedrooms, so that no-one had to go to bed in the dark; and if a man went out at night, he no longer bumped into his friends. The dwarfs came out of their caves in the mountains and ran races with the rabbits. The elves in their red pointed caps danced in rings on the village green.

The four brothers took care to see that the moon was kept clean and full

of oil, and was lit every night as the sun went down. For this the people were glad to give them six and eightpence a week.

Things went on like this until Arn, the old one, fell ill.

'One quarter of this moon belongs to me,' said he, 'and, if I die, I must have it to take to the grave with me.'

When Arn died, the Mayor climbed up the tree and snipped off one quarter of the moon with his hedge shears. As Arn's property, this was put in the coffin with him and buried.

The moon now gave a little less light, but still the nights were bright enough. Then, not long afterwards, Bor fell ill, and he too claimed a quarter of the moon as his share. So when Bor died, once more the Mayor climbed up the tree and cut off a second quarter of the moon with his hedge shears, and this was buried in Bor's coffin.

The light of the moon grew less; and it grew still less when Cass died, and the third quarter was cut off and placed in his coffin. Finally, when Deol died and took his quarter with him, there was no moon at all. The old state of darkness began again, and the people of Exe, if they went out at night without their lanterns, bumped their heads together.

But in the land below the earth, where dead men go and where it is always dark, the four pieces of the moon joined together. In the soft light, which now shone all the time, the dead began to feel restless. Astonished to find they could see again, they climbed out of their graves and were merry.

They began to behave as before,

dancing, singing and gathering in the taverns to drink and jest. As you can imagine, they drank too much, for they had long been unaccustomed to wine and ale. Some started to brawl and quarrel. They took up cudgels and began to attack each other.

The noise from the underworld grew louder and louder, and at last reached heaven. On hearing it, Saint Peter, who guards the gate of heaven, thought that a state of war must have broken out in the lower world. He summoned the Blessed Ones, whose duty it was to drive off the assaults of the Evil One. But the Blessed Ones did not come, so Saint Peter in a rage mounted his horse and rode out through the gate of heaven. He charged down to the lower world and, in a voice of thunder, ordered the dead to behave themselves and return to their graves.

He saw that the moon was the cause of all the trouble, so he slung it over his back, galloped off and hung it up in heaven; there, to this very day, it shines as brightly as ever.

This is a story by the Brothers Grimm, re-told by James Reeves.

In the Middle of the Night

In the middle of the night a fly woke
Charlie. At first he lay listening, half-
asleep, while it swooped about the
room. Sometimes it was far;
sometimes it was near – that was
what had woken him; and
occasionally it was very near indeed.
It was very, very near when the
buzzing stopped: the fly had alighted
on his face. He jerked his head up; the
fly buzzed off. Now he was really
awake.

The fly buzzed wildly about the
room, but it was thinking of Charlie

all the time. It swooped nearer and nearer. Nearer . . .

Charlie pulled his head down under the bedclothes. All of him under the bedclothes, he was completely protected; but he could hear nothing except his heartbeats and his breathing. He was overwhelmed by the smell of warm bedding, warm pyjamas, warm himself. He was going to suffocate. So he rose suddenly up out of the bedclothes; and the fly was waiting for him. It dashed at him. He beat it with his hands. At the same time he appealed to his younger brother, Wilson, in the next bed: 'Wilson, there's a fly!'

Wilson, unstirring, slept on.

Now Charlie and the fly were pitting their wits against each other: Charlie pouncing on the air where he thought the fly must be; the fly sliding under his guard towards his face. Again and again the fly reached Charlie; again and again, almost simultaneously, Charlie dislodged him. Once he hit the fly – or, at least, hit where the fly had been a second before, on the side of his head; the blow was so hard that his head sang with it afterwards.

Then suddenly the fight was over; no more buzzing. His blows – or rather, one of them – must have told.

He laid his head back on the pillow, thinking of going to sleep again. But he was also thinking of the fly, and now he noticed a tickling in the ear he turned to the pillow.

It must be – it *was* – the fly.

He rose in such a panic that the waking of Wilson really seemed to him a possible thing, and useful. He shook him repeatedly: 'Wilson –

Wilson, I tell you, there's a fly in my ear!'

Wilson groaned, turned over very slowly like a seal in water, and slept on.

The tickling in Charlie's ear continued. He could just imagine the fly struggling in some passageway too narrow for its wingspan. He longed to put his finger into his ear and rattle it round, like a stick in a rabbit-hole; but he was afraid of driving the fly deeper into his ear.

Wilson slept on.

Charlie stood in the middle of the bedroom floor, quivering and trying to think. He needed to see down his ear, or to get someone else to see down it. Wilson wouldn't do; perhaps Margaret would.

Margaret's room was next door. Charlie turned on the light as he entered: Margaret's bed was empty. He was startled, and then thought that she must have gone to the lavatory. But there was no light from there. He listened carefully: there was no sound from anywhere, except for the usual snuffling moans from the hall, where Floss slept and dreamt of dog-biscuits. The empty bed was mystifying; but Charlie had his ear to worry about. It sounded as if there were a pigeon inside it now.

Wilson asleep; Margaret vanished; that left Alison. But Alison was bossy, just because she was the eldest; and, anyway, she would probably only wake Mum. He might as well wake Mum himself.

Down the passage and through the door always left ajar. 'Mum,' he said. She woke, or at least half-woke, at once: 'Who is it? Who? Who?

What's the matter? What—?'

'I've a fly in my ear.'

'You can't have.'

'It flew in.'

She switched on the bedside light, and, as she did so, Dad plunged beneath the bedclothes with an exclamation and lay still again.

Charlie knelt at his mother's side of the bed and she looked into his ear. 'There's nothing.'

'Something crackles.'

'It's wax in your ear.'

'It tickles.'

'There's no fly there. Go back to bed and stop imagining things.'

His father's arm came up from below the bedclothes. The hand waved about, settled on the bedside light and clicked it out. There was an upheaval of bedclothes and a comfortable grunt.

'Good night,' said Mum from the darkness. She was already allowing herself to sink back into sleep again.

'Good night,' Charlie said sadly. Then an idea occurred to him. He repeated his good night loudly and added some coughing, to cover the fact that he was closing the bedroom door behind him – the door that Mum kept open so that she could listen for her children. They had outgrown all that kind of attention, except possibly for Wilson. Charlie had shut the door against Mum's hearing because he intended to slip downstairs for a drink of water – well, for a drink and perhaps a snack. That fly-business had woken him up and also weakened him: he needed something.

He crept downstairs, trusting to Floss's good sense not to make a row. He turned the foot of the staircase towards the kitchen, and there had not been the faintest whimper from her, far less a bark. He was passing the dog-basket when he had the most unnerving sensation of something being wrong there – something unusual, at least. He could not have said whether he had heard something or smelt something – he could certainly have seen nothing in the blackness: perhaps some extra sense warned him.

'Floss?' he whispered, and there was the usual little scrabble and snuffle. He held out his fingers low down for Floss to lick. As she did not do so at once, he moved them towards her, met some obstruction—

'Don't poke your fingers in my eye!' a voice said, very low-toned and cross. Charlie's first, confused thought was that Floss had spoken:

the voice was familiar – but then a voice from Floss should *not* be familiar; it should be strangely new to him—

He took an uncertain little step towards the voice, tripped over the obstruction, which was quite wrong in shape and size to be Floss, and sat down. Two things now happened. Floss, apparently having climbed over the obstruction, reached his lap and began to lick his face. At the same time a human hand fumbled over his face, among the slappings of Floss's tongue, and settled over his mouth. 'Don't make a row! Keep quiet!' said the voice. Charlie's mind cleared: he knew, although without understanding, that he was sitting on the floor in the dark with Floss on his knee and Margaret beside him.

Her hand came off his mouth.

'What are you doing here, anyway, Charlie?'

'I like that! What about you? There was a fly in my ear.'

'Go on!'

'There was.'

'Why does that make you come downstairs?'

'I wanted a drink of water.'

'There's water in the bathroom.'

'Well, I'm a bit hungry.'

'If Mum catches you . . .'

'Look here,' Charlie said, 'you tell me what you're doing down here.'

Margaret sighed. 'Just sitting with Floss.'

'You can't come down and just sit with Floss in the middle of the night.'

'Yes, I can. I keep her company. Only at weekends, of course. No-one seemed to realize what it was like for her when those puppies went. She just

159

couldn't get to sleep for loneliness.'

'But the last puppy went weeks ago. You haven't been keeping Floss company every Saturday night since then.'

'Why not?'

Charlie gave up. 'I'm going to get my food and drink,' he said. He went into the kitchen, followed by Margaret, followed by Floss.

They all had a quick drink of water. Then Charlie and Margaret looked into the larder: the remains of a joint; a very large quantity of mashed potato; most of a loaf; eggs; butter; cheese . . .

'I suppose it'll have to be just bread and butter and a bit of cheese,' said Charlie. 'Else Mum might notice.'

'Something hot,' said Margaret. 'I'm cold from sitting in the hall comforting Floss. I need hot cocoa, I think.' She poured some milk into a saucepan and put it on the hotplate. Then she began to search for the tin of cocoa. Charlie, standing by the cooker, was already absorbed in the making of a rough cheese sandwich.

The milk in the pan began to steam. Given time, it rose in the saucepan, peered over the top, and boiled over on to the hotplate, where it sizzled loudly. Margaret rushed back and pulled the saucepan to one side. 'Well, really, Charlie! Now there's that awful smell! It'll still be here in the morning, too.'

'Set the fan going,' Charlie suggested.

The fan drew the smell from the cooker up and away through a pipe to the outside. It also made a loud roaring noise. Not loud enough to reach their parents, who slept on the other side of the house – that was all that Charlie and Margaret thought of.

Alison's bedroom, however, was immediately above the kitchen. Charlie was eating his bread and cheese, Margaret was drinking her cocoa, when the kitchen door opened and there stood Alison. Only Floss was pleased to see her.

'Well!' she said.

Charlie muttered something about a fly in his ear, but Margaret said nothing. Alison had caught them red-handed. She would call Mum downstairs, that was obvious. There would be an awful row.

Alison stood there. She liked commanding a situation.

Then, instead of taking a step backwards to call up the stairs to Mum, she took a step forward into the kitchen. 'What are you having, anyway?' she asked. She glanced with scorn at Charlie's poor piece of bread and cheese and at Margaret's cocoa. She moved over to the larder, flung open the door, and looked searchingly inside. In such a way must Napoleon have viewed a battlefield before the victory.

Her gaze fell upon the bowl of mashed potato. 'I shall make potato-cakes,' said Alison.

They watched while she brought the mashed potato to the kitchen table. She switched on the oven, fetched her other ingredients, and began mixing.

'Mum'll notice if you take much of that potato,' said Margaret.

But Alison thought big. 'She may notice if some potato is missing,' she agreed. 'But if there's none at all, and if the bowl it was in is washed and dried and stacked away with the others, then she's going to think she must have made a mistake. There just can never have been any mashed potato.'

Alison rolled out her mixture and cut it into cakes; then she set the cakes on a baking-tin and put it in the oven.

Now she did the washing-up. Throughout the time they were in the kitchen, Alison washed up and put away as she went along. She wanted no-one's help. She was very methodical, and she did everything herself to be sure that nothing was left undone. In the morning there must be no trace left of the cooking in the middle of the night.

'And now,' said Alison, 'I think we should fetch Wilson.'

The other two were aghast at the

idea; but Alison was firm in her reasons. 'It's better if we're all in this together, Wilson as well. Then, if the worst comes to the worst, it won't be just us three caught out, with Wilson hanging on to Mum's apron-strings, smiling innocence. We'll all be for it together; and Mum'll be softer with us if we've got Wilson.'

They saw that, at once. But Margaret still objected: 'Wilson will tell. He just always tells everything. He can't help it.'

Alison said, 'He always tells everything. Right: we'll give him something *to* tell, and then see if Mum believes him. We'll do an entertainment for him. Get an umbrella from the hall and Wilson's sou'wester and a blanket or a rug or something. Go on.'

They would not obey Alison's

orders until they had heard her plan;
then they did. They fetched the
umbrella and the hat, and lastly they
fetched Wilson, still sound asleep,
slung between the two of them in his
eiderdown. They propped him in a
chair at the kitchen table, where he
still slept.

By now the potato-cakes were
done. Alison took them out of the
oven and set them on the table before
Wilson. She buttered them, handing
them in turn to Charlie and Margaret
and helping herself. One was set aside
to cool for Floss.

The smell of fresh-cooked, buttery
potato-cake woke Wilson, as was to
be expected. First his nose sipped the
air, then his eyes opened, his gaze
settled on the potato-cakes.

'Like one?' Alison asked.

Wilson opened his mouth wide and

Alison put a potato-cake inside, whole.

'They're paradise-cakes,' Alison said.

'Potato-cakes?' said Wilson, recognizing the taste.

'No, paradise-cakes, Wilson,' and then, stepping aside, she gave him a clear view of Charlie's and Margaret's entertainment, with the umbrella and the sou'wester hat and his eiderdown. 'Look, Wilson, look.'

Wilson watched with wide-open eyes, and into his wide-open mouth Alison put, one by one, the potato-cakes that were his share.

But, as they had foreseen, Wilson did not stay awake for very long. When there were no more potato-cakes, he yawned, drowsed, and suddenly was deeply asleep. Charlie and Margaret put him back into his eiderdown and took him upstairs to bed. They came down to return the umbrella and the sou'wester to their proper places, and to see Floss back into her basket. Alison, last out of the kitchen, made sure that everything was in its place.

The next morning Mum was down first. On Sunday she always cooked a proper breakfast for anyone there in time. Dad was always there in time; but this morning Mum was still looking for a bowl of mashed potato when he appeared.

'I can't think where it's gone,' she said. 'I can't think.'

'I'll have the bacon and eggs without the potato,' said Dad; and he did. While he ate, Mum went back to searching.

Wilson came down, and was sent upstairs again to put on a dressing-gown. On his return he said that

Charlie was still asleep and there was no sound from the girls' rooms either. He said he thought they were tired out. He went on talking while he ate his breakfast. Dad was reading the paper and Mum had gone back to poking about in the larder for the bowl of mashed potato, but Wilson liked talking even if no-one would listen. When Mum came out of the larder for a moment, still without her potato, Wilson was saying: '. . . And Charlie sat in an umbrella-boat on an eiderdown-sea, and Margaret pretended to be a sea-serpent, and Alison gave us paradise-cakes to eat. Floss had one too, but it was too hot for her. What are paradise-cakes? Dad, what's a paradise-cake?'

'Don't know,' said Dad, reading.

'Mum, what's a paradise-cake?'

'Oh, Wilson, don't bother so when

I'm looking for something . . . When did you eat this cake, anyway?'

'I told you. Charlie sat in his umbrella-boat on an eiderdown-sea and Margaret was a sea-serpent and Alison—'

'Wilson,' said his mother, 'you've been dreaming.'

'No, really – really!' Wilson cried.

But his mother paid no further attention. 'I give up,' she said. 'That mashed potato: it must have been last weekend . . .' She went out of the kitchen to call the others: 'Charlie! Margaret! Alison!'

Wilson, in the kitchen, said to his father, 'I wasn't dreaming. And Charlie said there was a fly in his ear.'

Dad had been quarter-listening; now he put down his paper. 'What?'

'Charlie had a fly in his ear.'

Dad stared at Wilson. 'And what did you say that Alison fed you with?'

'Paradise-cakes. She'd just made them, I think, in the middle of the night.'

'What were they like?'

'Lovely. Hot, with butter. Lovely.'

'But were they – well, could they have had any mashed potato in them, for instance?'

In the hall Mum was finishing her calling: 'Charlie! Margaret! Alison! I warn you now!'

'I don't know about that,' Wilson said. 'They were paradise-cakes. They tasted a bit like the potato-cakes Mum makes, but Alison said they weren't. She specially said they were paradise-cakes.'

Dad nodded. 'You've finished your breakfast. Go up and get dressed, and you can take this,' he took a coin from his pocket, 'straight off to the sweet-shop. Go on.'

Mum met Wilson at the kitchen door: 'Where's he off to in such a hurry?'

'I gave him something to buy sweets with,' said Dad. 'I wanted a quiet breakfast. He talks too much.'

This story is by Philippa Pearce.

A SATCHEL OF SCHOOL STORIES
Collected by Pat Thomson

Unpack this satchel of stories and pull out . . . a Pet Afternoon that ends in chaos, an uproarious class trip to the Safari Park, a dog who becomes a teacher, a strange new classmate who can see into the future and a whole host of other fascinating and exciting characters. You won't want to stop reading until you get right to the bottom of the satchel!

'Picking the right audience for each of the stories will ensure an enjoyable experience and encourage language skills . . . an invaluable source of material for reading to classes'
The Junior Bookshelf

0 552 527386

CORGI BOOKS

A BAND OF JOINING-IN STORIES
Collected by Pat Thomson

A great, action-packed collection
of stories!

There are rhythms to clap along with,
actions to copy, animal noises and
repeated choruses as young listeners
join in with a lion hunt, discover
Rajah's big secret – and even
outwit a fearsome troll!

'Great fun'
School Librarian

0 552 528253

CORGI BOOKS